Louis
the Lifeboat

Nasty Black Stuff
The

RAVETTE PUBLISHING

D0785755

Louis the Lifeboat
© 2002 Tandem Licensing and Media Ltd.

Created by Frank Bell & Colin Bowler

Written by Gordon Volke

Illustrated by Colin Bowler

First published by Ravette Publishing 2002

Ravette Publishing Limited

Unit 3, Tristar Centre, Star Road, Partridge Green,
West Sussex RH13 8RA

ISBN: 1 84161 119 0

One evening, Jack arrived in the bathroom with a bag that went CHINK, CHINK, CHINK!

"What have you got there?" asked mum.

"These are my new bath toys!" chuckled Jack.

Every evening, Jack plays a game in the bath. He imagines his toy lifeboat, Louis, having adventures in Sunshine Bay ...

It was a lovely day.
The sky was blue, the sea
was calm and Louis' radio
was quiet. So the little
lifeboat should have felt
happy.

But, instead, he felt
worried.

"It's too quiet,"
he murmured.

Suddenly, Louis realised
what was wrong. Stanley the
Seagull, who always flew
down for a chat, had not
appeared today.

"Wonder where he's
got to?" cried Louis.

Louis asked his friend, Pierre, if he had seen Stanley.
"No, I 'ave not seen zat chatterbox seagull!" replied
the French fishing boat. "He is not around."
"How strange!" murmured Louis.

The lifeboat sped away before Pierre
had a chance to say any more.
"Zut alors!" grumbled the fishing boat.
"Why are ze English always in a 'urry?
I 'ave not warned Louis about zat
dangerous place ..."

Louis was sure that something had happened to Stanley. He searched the Bay, calling the seagull's name, and at last he heard a faint cry in the distance.

"It's coming from Seagull Rock!" exclaimed Louis.

The lifeboat found his friend on the rock, unable to fly.

"It's my wing, old boy!" squawked Stanley. "It's covered with this nasty black stuff!"

The injured seagull managed to flutter onto Louis' deck.

"While I remember," he cried, "I must warn you about a very dangerous place ..."
But Louis cut him short.

"Can't gossip now, Stanley," he said. "You must get to a vet and have that black stuff washed off with soapy water."

When Stanley was safe, Louis went to see Grace, the lighthouse who watched over Sunshine Bay.

"What IS this nasty black stuff?" asked Louis.

"Oil!" replied the lighthouse. "It's leaking from the tanker that sank last year."

Louis imagined the oil being washed up on the beaches.

"Everything would be ruined!" he cried. So the little lifeboat sped off to look for more oil floating in the sea.

Grace was cross that Louis left so quickly.
"I need to warn him about Seashell Head.
It's looking very dangerous."
But Louis was too far away to hear
the lighthouse's calls.

Seashell Head was a long piece of land that stuck out into the sea. Louis was just passing it when SPLOOOSH! A huge rock toppled into the water beside him.
"HEY!" yelled Louis. "That nearly sank me!"

Louis looked up at the headland and gasped in horror. There had been a big landslide and lots more huge rocks were about to fall into the sea.

"I must warn all passing ships!" exclaimed Louis.

Louis started to turn ... and then stopped.
He could not move through the water!
And, looking down, he found that the sea had
turned black!

"Oil!" he gasped in horror. "And it's heading
for Sunshine Bay!"

What could Louis do to stop the oil
sweeping into the Bay? There was no time to
radio for help, so he had to act on his own.

"I know!" he exclaimed, looking up at the
loose rocks on Seashell Head.

Louis sailed clear of the headland. Then he sounded his powerful foghorns over and over again. PARP, PARP they went, making everything shake. Soon, the mass of piled-up rocks began to move!

SPLISH! SPLASH! SPLOSH! One by one, the giant rocks rolled into the sea. Soon, they stretched out across the entrance to the Bay like a wall.

"But will it be in time?" wondered Louis.

18

The oil slick swept in on the tide and
was stopped by the barrier of stones.
Now the nasty black stuff could not reach
the beaches and spoil them!

"Bravo, Louis!" cheered Pierre, who had come to join his friend. "Sometimes it is good to be fast, yes?"

Stanley also joined Louis. His wing was clean and he could fly again.

"The news is," croaked the seagull, excitedly, "that the Mayor has promised to get rid of this horrid oil once and for all. So it'll never trouble us again!"

"HURRAY!" cheered Louis.

21

In the bathroom, mum spotted Jack tipping
marbles into his water.
"You can't play marbles in the bath, Jack!"
she cried.
"These are rocks, mum!" replied Jack.
"Louis is saving Sunshine Bay!"
"Whatever next?" laughed mum.